from an idea by Andrea Dami

Illustrations by: Marco Campanella
Text by: Anna Casalis
Design by: Stefania Pavin

ISBN 1-84135-343-4

Illustrations © 2003 Dami Editore
English/UK text copyright © 2004 Award Publications Ltd

This edition first published 2004

First published 2004
Second impression 2005

Published by Award Publications Limited,
The Old Riding School, Welbeck Estate,
Worksop, Nottinghamshire S80 3LR

Printed in China

Billy Brownmouse
Won't Go To Sleep!

English text by Jackie Andrews
Illustrated by Marco Campanella

AWARD PUBLICATIONS LIMITED

It was early evening, and Billy Brownmouse was enjoying his supper. His teddy bear, Stilton, was waiting for him to finish. Stilton didn't eat supper.

"Mmmm!" said Billy B, licking his whiskers. "Cream cheese is my very favourite." He looked into his empty bowl. "What a pity it's all gone."

It was time for bed. Billy B changed into his special smiley-moon nightshirt. "Ooof!" he said, as he struggled to put it on. It was getting a bit tight for him now. Stilton sat patiently by the bed: he didn't wear a nightshirt.

Plink!

Next, Billy B had to clean his teeth. He brushed them carefully, up and down, up and down.

"Mmmm!" he said, "this toothpaste tastes delicious!"

Stilton leaned against the toothpaste tube: he didn't have any teeth to clean.

Then Billy B washed his face and paws, and scrubbed his whiskers.

At last he was ready for bed.

Billy B snuggled down under his thick, warm quilt with Stilton beside him.

"Mama!" he called. "I'm ready! Will you read me a story? I'd like a nice scary story, please!"

Tucked up in bed, with Stilton at his side and the light on, Billy B felt very brave.

Mama Brownmouse came and sat by Billy's
bed and opened the book of bedtime stories:
"Once upon a time," she began.

Once upon a time···

But before Mama Brownmouse reached the end of the story, she began to yawn and closed the book. "That's enough for now," she said. "You must go to sleep." "But what happens next?" asked Billy. "Does the hero escape? What happens to the Big Bad Cat?" "Not now, Billy B," said his mama. "I'll finish it tomorrow."

Mama Brownmouse kissed Billy B goodnight and went off to get ready for bed. But Billy wasn't at all sleepy, and after a while he got out of bed.

"Come on Stilton," he said.
"Let's go and find mama."

Billy's mama and papa were already in bed. Mama Brownmouse was reading a book, but Papa Brownmouse was asleep. He had to get up early in the morning.

"Mama," said Billy B, "I'm thirsty. May I have a drink, please?"

Stilton, of course, never needed a drink.

Glug-glug

After finishing a whole bottle of milk, Billy went back to bed.

He lay for a while staring up at the ceiling. "Lying in bed is very boring, Stilton," he said. "Nothing interesting ever happens."

Ahhh

Billy B didn't want to go to sleep.

He picked up Stilton again and went back to his mama and papa's room.

Mama Brownmouse had put her book away and had switched off the light. Papa Brownmouse was sound asleep and snoring lightly, his long whiskers vibrating with each snore.

"Mama," whispered Billy B. "Why do I have to go to sleep? It's such a waste of time!"

Mama yawned and got out of bed. She picked up Billy B and carried him over to the window.

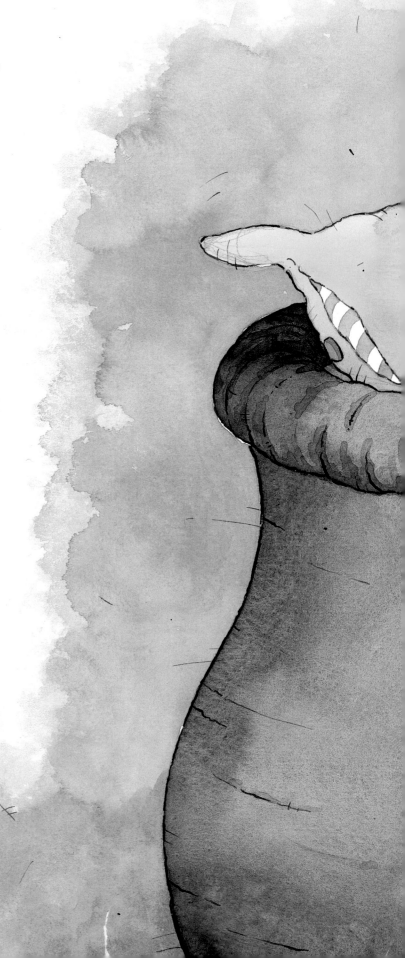

Mama...

"Look outside, Billy," she said. "The sun has gone to bed and it's very dark, so that little mice and other creatures of the day can sleep and rest, and maybe dream of good things. Then in the morning they will wake up happy and ready for a new day."

So Billy B went back to bed and was soon fast asleep… and dreaming.

Billy B dreamed he and Stilton were jumping up and down on a huge slice of tasty cheese. All around them were marvellous toys and delicious things to eat. He and Stilton had a wonderful time!

Yippee!

The sun streamed into Billy B's room next morning and woke him up. It was a lovely day.

"Come on, Stilton!" he said, jumping out of bed. "It's a great day. I can't wait to tell my friends at nursery school all about my wonderful dream. What a good job we went to sleep after all!"